To Clara

I hope you enjoy
Josephine's story.
Happy Trails

Roni McFadd

Josephine

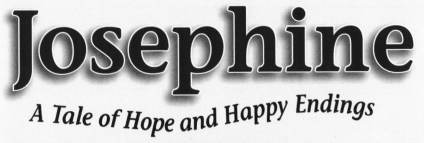

A Tale of Hope and Happy Endings

based on a true story

Bunny McLeod and Roni McFadden
Illustrated by Sierra Gaston

THE BISCUIT PRESS

Josephine

A Tale of Hope and Happy Endings

Copyright © 2010 Roni McFadden

The Biscuit Press
Address: 16250 Blue Jay Ln, Willits, CA 95490
Tel: 707-391-5461
Fax: 707-485-7904

Published in association with Jacqueline Cooper, American Legend Horse Farm, and underwritten by Mendocino County Farm Supply.

Illustrations by Sierra Gaston

Cover and book design by Michael Brechner/Cypress House

PUBLISHER'S CATALOGING-IN-PUBLICATION DATA

Manufactured by Friesens Corporation in Altona, MB, Canada

October 2010
Job #59550

McFadden, Roni.
   Josephine : a tale of hope and happy endings / by Roni McFadden
and Bunny McLeod. -- 1st ed. --Willits, CA : The Biscuit Press, c2010.
    p. ; cm.
   ISBN: 978-0-9844883-9-1

Audience: This is a read-aloud book for ages 4 and up.

Summary: At just four days of age, Josephine, a great-granddaughter of the famous racehorse Seabiscuit, loses her mother. Josephine's struggle for survival hinges on her caretakers finding a surrogate mother to nurture her. The touching story, told from the little filly's perspective, portrays the doubts and uncertainties a young orphan feels as she faces the prospect of going on without the most important individual in her young life, her mother.

1. Horses--Juvenile literature. 2. Horses--Care--Juvenile literature. I. McLeod, Bunny. II. Title.

   SF291 .M34 2010   636.1--dc22 1005

Printed in Canada
2 4 6 8 9 7 5 3
FIRST EDITION

This book is dedicated
to Josephine's ancestor,

Seabiscuit

and to all of the underdogs who have
overcome adversity against all odds.

Josephine looked all around. She had just barely been born, and she had landed right in the arms of a lady named Jacqueline who petted her gently and seemed very happy to see her. She could hear people talking excitedly. They seemed very happy to see her too.

Suddenly, Josephine heard a very special sound. It was a special nicker, you know, the love sound that mother horses and baby horses make to each other, and Josephine thought it was the most beautiful sound she could imagine. She knew that whoever had made that love sound loved her very much, and she quickly made the love sound right back.

Josephine looked up right into the eyes of a big golden-colored horse. The big horse's eyes were filled with a special love look that Josephine knew was just for her. "Your name is Josephine," the big horse told her. "I am your mother. My name is Lacy. You have a special name for me. You call me Mama."

The big horse reached down and
rubbed her head against the
side of little Josephine's face,
and then gave her a big kiss. "Josie,
Josie, Josephine," the Mama Lacy
horse sang softly. Josephine thought
that was the most beautiful song in
the whole world.
Everything seemed absolutely perfect
in little Josephine's world, and she
was a very happy little horse.

Then, suddenly everything changed. The Mama Lacy horse became very sick. The people who were there tried to help, but the Mama Lacy horse was still very sick. The Jacqueline lady who owned the Mama Lacy horse and little Josephine called the doctor.

The doctor came right away and gave the Mama Lacy horse some medicine, but it didn't make her better. The doctor said she would have to go to the hospital, so the people put her in a trailer to take her there. They let little Josephine go with her.

When they got to the hospital, the doctors were waiting for them. They all tried very hard to help the Mama Lacy horse get better, but it just didn't happen. The doctors took the Mama Lacy horse away from where little Josephine was, and she never came back, not ever.

Josephine listened to the people talk. She heard them use the word "died" and she heard enough to learn that this meant that the Mama Lacy horse had gotten so sick that finally her spirit left her body to go to a wonderful place where she would be happy and never be sick again. Josephine was very glad for the Mama Lacy horse that she wasn't sick anymore, but she was very sad for herself.

Josephine missed the Mama Lacy horse very much, and wished that she could come back and sing the "Josie, Josie, Josephine" song to her, just one more time. "Josie, Josie, Josephine," she sang softly to herself. She still thought it was the most wonderful song in the world, but it just wasn't the same when she sang it to herself as it was when the Mama Lacy horse had sung it to her.

A big tear rolled down from Josephine's left eye and splashed onto the floor. Little Josephine missed the Mama Lacy horse very, very much, and she felt very, very sad.

The people at the hospital taught Josephine to drink milk from a bucket and also from a bottle. The milk tasted very good, and it filled the big hungry place in Josephine's tummy.

The Jacqueline lady came to see Josephine every day and petted her and hugged her. Josephine could see the special love look in the Jacqueline lady's eyes, and she knew it was for her. This made her feel happy.

She wished that she and the Jacqueline lady spoke the same language so that she could teach the lady the Josie, Josie, Josephine song. She had a feeling that if the Jacqueline lady knew the Josie, Josie, Josephine song and how much Josephine liked it, she would sing it to her often.

Josephine heard the doctors and the Jacqueline lady and other people talk about something called a surrogate mother. She knew that it had something to do with her, but she didn't know what. Whatever a surrogate mother was, Josephine knew that they were having a hard time finding one.

One day the Jacqueline lady came. She had the trailer that she had used to bring the Mama Lacy horse and Josephine to the hospital. She put Josephine in the trailer. "For now you can live in the barn right next to the house where I live," she told her.

When they got to the farm, the Jacqueline lady opened the back of the trailer so that Josephine could come out.

Suddenly, Josephine heard a very special sound. It was the special love sound that mother horses and baby horses make to each other. Quickly, Josephine called back and looked all around. She looked up right into the eyes of a big black-and-white horse, whose eyes were filled with a special love look that Josephine knew was just for her.

"I know who you are," the big horse told Josephine.
"Your name is Josephine."

"That's right," said Josephine. "But I don't know who you are. You're not my mother. The Mama Lacy horse is my mother, and she had to go far away."

"That's right," said the big black-and-white horse. She leaned down and gave Josephine a big kiss and rubbed her head on the side of Josephine's little face, very much like the Mama Lacy horse had done. "I heard the Jacqueline lady and the other people talking about it. They said that the Lacy horse was very sick and that finally her spirit had left her body and gone to a wonderful place where she will never be sick again. Someday, when the time is right, you will go there and be with her."

"I will?" brightened Josephine. "Will she remember me?"

"Oh, yes," said the big horse. "She loves you very much, you know, and we never forget those we love."

"Will she sing the Josie, Josie, Josephine song to me?" asked Josephine.

"I'm sure she will," the big horse smiled. "I'm absolutely sure she will."

"But you made a mistake. You said that I am not your mother. Well, it's true that I am not your Lacy mother. She is your first mother. I am your second mother. My name is Midnight, but you have a special name for me—you call me Mama. You are a very lucky little filly because now you have two mothers instead of one. The Lacy horse will always be your first mother, just the same as always, but now I am your mother too.

Josephine looked into the Midnight horse's eyes. She could see the love that was there and knew that it was all for her. It didn't look exactly the same as the Lacy Mama's love had looked because it came from the Midnight Mama's love, but it was a very special love—and it was all for Josephine.

"Do you know the Josie, Josie, Josephine song?" asked Josephine hopefully.

"No, I don't, but if you'll teach it to me I'll sing it to you. It sounds like a very nice song."

Josephine sang the Josie, Josie, Josephine song for the Midnight Mama, and the Midnight Mama listened carefully.

Then Midnight sang softly to her new little daughter, "Josie, Josie, Josephine."

Josephine felt very happy.
She thought it was the most beautiful song in the whole wide world.

Bunny McLeod, coauthor

Bunny McLeod is a seventy-year-old who, although she has written all her life, began her official career as a writer in 2005 at age sixty-five, right after graduating with an honors degree in sociology from New England College in Henniker, New Hampshire. She is the coauthor of the international best-selling children's book *Who Says Kids Can't Fight Global Warming*, written with Patrick Harrison, *Christmas in Distress*, written with A. L. Niflhaim, and a science-fiction book, *Probed by Aliens*, written with Van Strickland. She has also written more than seventy books for the Korean publishing company GlenndomanKorea, and is one of the most popular children's authors in Korea.

Roni McFadden, coauthor

Roni McFadden is a mother of four and grandmother of thirteen who lives in Willits, California, on property that was once part of the Ridgewood Ranch, home of Seabiscuit, where Josephine now resides. For twenty years Roni has worked for the equine vets who care for the horses at the ranch. She has been around horses all her life, and will soon publish her story, *Sierra Lady,* about her teenage years at a pack station in the High Sierra. She is excited to be a part of this philanthropic project and is eager to see the results.

Sierra Gaston, Illustrator

Sierra Gaston lives in northern California and is a student at Mendocino College. She loves horses, books, and art, and is pursuing a bachelor's degree in illustration/visual media. Sierra feels honored to contribute to the legacy of the legendary racehorse Seabiscuit.

About American Legend Horse Farm

Jacqueline Cooper and her husband, Tim, own and operate American Legend Horse Farm, a modest horse-breeding farm in Redwood Valley, California. Specializing in the rare bloodline of Seabiscuit, the couple hopes to someday race one of their Thoroughbreds descended from the legendary racehorse. Stabled at historic Ridgewood Ranch, the home of the champion in Willits, California, the Lil'Biscuits, as they are known, are available for viewing during seasonal ranch tours. To learn more about American Legend Horse Farm, visit www.legendhorse.com.

Photo by Maureen Moore, *The Willits News*

Josephine, a registered Paint filly (APHA reg. Champs Lil'Biscuit), is the first descendant of Seabiscuit born at the historic Howard mare barn in over fifty years. She is descended from Seabiscuit through her dam First Class Lacegold, affectionately known as Lacy.

All proceeds from the sale of this book
are in support of the following:

Ridgewood T.R.A.I.L. Riders Association
Ridgewood Ranch, Willits, California

T.R.A.I.L. is a nonprofit 501 (c) 3 therapeutic riding program and member of NARHA, established in 1993 at historic Ridgewood Ranch, the home of the legendary racehorse Seabiscuit. The program provides services to improve the lives of children and adults challenged physically, developmentally, emotionally, and socially.

For donor and volunteer opportunities,
or to participate in the program, please contact:

Ridgewood T.R.A.I.L. Riders, Assoc.
16200 N. Hwy 101 • Willits, CA. 95490
Tel.: (707) 456-9202 (message)
Erin Livingston, Instructor • Tel.: (707)391-3873

The Frank R. Howard Foundation
www.howardfoundation.org

Charles S. Howard, owner of the famed racehorse Seabiscuit, donated funds for a hospital to be built in the rural community of Willits, California, in response to the tragic loss of his son, Frank R. Howard. Young Frank suffered a severe accident in a remote area outside Willits, with no hospital near enough to save his life. Since 1928, Frank R. Howard Memorial Hospital has served the community of Willits and northern Mendocino County with distinction.

The Frank R. Howard Foundation is currently raising funds for a new Howard Hospital campus and wellness center in Willits.

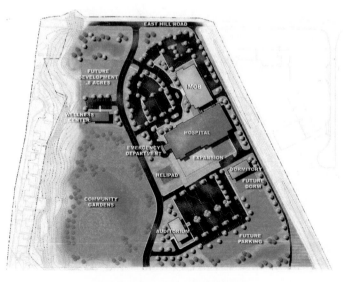

Medical Campus Plan